"You won't hear a peep out of me, kid,"
promised T.R. Bear when Jimmy decided to
take him to school for show and tell. The
trouble was that T.R. was a rather excitable
bear and he tended to break the rules . . .

This is the second in a series of books about
T.R. Bear, written by Terrance Dicks, the
best-selling author of *Dr Who*.

T.R. Bear

T.R. GOES TO SCHOOL

T.R. BEAR

T.R. Goes To School

Terrance Dicks
Illustrated by
Susan Hellard

YOUNG CORGI BOOKS

T.R. BEAR
T.R. GOES TO SCHOOL
A YOUNG CORGI BOOK   0 552 52302X

PRINTING HISTORY
First published in Great Britain by Piccadilly Press
Piccadilly Press edition published 1985
Young Corgi edition published 1986
Reprinted 1987, 1988

Young Corgi Books are published by Transworld Publishers Ltd.,
61-63 Uxbridge Road, Ealing, London W5 5SA, in Australia by
Transworld Publishers (Australia) Pty. Ltd., 15-23 Helles
Avenue, Moorebank, NSW 2170, and in New Zealand by
Transworld Publishers (N.Z.) Ltd., Cnr. Moselle
and Waipareira Avenues, Henderson, Auckland.

Made and printed in Great Britain by
The Guernsey Press Co. Ltd., Guernsey, Channel Islands.

Chapter One

T.R. Makes a Complaint

Jimmy was sitting on a bench in the park, talking to his teddy bear.

'Come on, kid, gimme a break,' pleaded T.R. Bear. 'I'm going crazy in that bedroom.'

'You've got Edward Bear and Sally Ann to talk to,' said Jimmy.

'Listen, I've got nothing against Edward and Sally Ann,' said T.R.

1

hurriedly. 'Great guys, great guys both of them.'

Edward was another teddy bear that Jimmy had had since he was very small. Sally Ann was a rag doll, originally belonging to Jimmy's sister Jenny.

Both toys now sat on the toy shelf in Jimmy's room, with T.R., the newcomer, between them.

Jimmy and T.R. fell silent as two old ladies toddled past.

'Look,' whispered one of them to her friend. 'That little boy's having a long conversation with his teddy bear. Isn't that sweet? Such imagination they have at that age! Rather an odd looking bear, though!'

T.R. opened his mouth to speak, but Jimmy clamped a hand over his muzzle. 'Sssh! Remember the rules!'

'Okay, okay,' mumbled T.R. 'No need to suffocate a guy.'

The two old ladies had narrowly escaped a nasty shock. The thing about T.R. Bear was, he really could talk – when he wanted to. So can all toys of course, but the rules about talking are very strict. No moving or talking unless the humans are asleep and the toys are alone.

The trouble was that T.R. was rather an excitable bear, and he tended to break the rules rather a lot. Perhaps it was because he was American – a fact which also accounted for what the old lady had rather unkindly called his odd appearance.

Most bears look cute and cuddly, but T.R. was tough. He was short and stocky and he wore a check shooting jacket and a red bow tie. Perhaps the most unusual thing about T.R. was the pair of round wire glasses perched on the end of his nose. They were secured by a ribbon of black silk.

There wasn't actually any glass in the spectacles but they were very important to T.R. They were part of his image. T.R.'s full name was

Theodore Roosevelt Bear and he modelled his appearance and his character on that long-ago American President who, according to T.R., had given his name to all teddy bears everywhere.

Like his famous namesake, T.R. Bear was small and rather short-sighted, but he was also very determined. T.R. was an All-American Bear, a go-getter, a hustler, a bear who got things done. Which, of course, was why he found life on the toy shelf a bit dull.

With the two old ladies safely out of sight, T.R. went on with his complaint. 'Like I say, Edward's a great guy, a truly wonderful bear, but he does kinda go on about his aristocratic connections.'

Edward secretly believed all teddy bears were really British, named after King Edward the Seventh.

'As for Sally Ann, I really respect her attitude to Doll's Lib. Trouble is, sometimes she can't seem to talk about anything else. I need variety, kid, new faces, new places.'

Jimmy had an inspiration. 'Well, tomorrow's Monday – it's show and tell day in school.'

'Come again, kid?'

'Show and tell. You bring something interesting to your class, show it to them and tell them all about it.'

'Well?'

'I could bring *you*,' said Jimmy. 'I could show you to the class, tell them how you arrived in a parcel from my uncle in America. I could tell them all about Teddy Roosevelt giving his name to the first teddy bears.'

T.R. sat back, nodding, holding the lapels of his jacket. 'Say, that could be pretty interesting at that. You English kids ought to get the straight stuff about teddy bears from somebody. Edward the Seventh my foot!'

'You'd have to let me do all the talking,' said Jimmy. 'They might be able to take American teddy bears, but a talking bear would be just too much!'

'You won't hear a peep outta me,'

promised T.R. 'I'll just sit there looking distinguished, while you do the honours.'

Suddenly they heard the sound of a frantic yelping. 'Oh dear, sighed Jimmy. 'Sounds like Harbottle's in trouble again.'

Harbottle was Jimmy's dog, a large shaggy shapeless beast with a rather mixed-up nature.

Harbottle looked very fierce, and sometimes liked to act as if he *was* fierce. But in fact, Harbottle was rather timid.

He was dashing towards them across the park, hotly pursued by an enormous black Alsatian.

Harbottle reached the bench and shot underneath it. Seconds later the Alsatian arrived.

One of T.R.'s stubby legs shot out

and his foot tapped the dog sharply
on the end of the nose.

'Scram,' boomed T.R. 'Go on, beat
it!'

With a yelp of alarm, the Alsatian
turned and fled.

'Well done T.R.!' said Jimmy.

T.R. chuckled. 'Walk softly, and
carry a big stick!' He grinned at
Jimmy. 'One of Teddy Roosevelt's
favourite sayings. Means don't go
starting trouble, but be ready to
handle it if it comes. Someone should

teach it to that pooch of yours.'

Jimmy looked at his watch. 'Time to be going home for lunch.' He picked up T.R. and set off, Harbottle loping behind.

'Now don't forget,' rumbled T.R. from underneath Jimmy's arm. 'You're taking me to school tomorrow, that's a deal, right?'

'All right,' said Jimmy. 'It's a deal. But don't expect too much. A day at school can be pretty dull!'

The way things turned out, T.R.'s day at school was anything but dull.

In fact, it turned out to be one of the most eventful days of Jimmy's life.

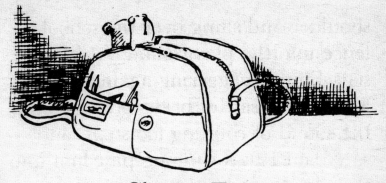

Chapter Two

A Trip for T.R.

Next morning, Monday, T.R. rode to school in Jimmy's school bag.

'Now remember,' said Jimmy as they neared the school gates. 'Leave the talking to me.'

T.R.'s voice came from inside the bag. 'Don't worry kid, there won't be a peep out of me. I'll be as quiet as an – aargh!'

The 'aargh!' came because the bag had been snatched from Jimmy's

shoulder and slung over the school
fence into the playground. A shove
sent Jimmy staggering against the
fence. He heard a braying laugh and
the sound of running footsteps, and
saw Paul Ferris running past him into
the playground.

Paul Ferris was the biggest, not to
say fattest, boy in Jimmy's class and
the nearest thing they had to a class
bully. Perhaps bully was putting it a
bit too strong, Paul never really hurt
anybody. But he was always playing
stupid practical tricks, like throwing
Jimmy's satchel, then running away.
He refused to do any real work in

12

class and sometimes he mucked about
so much that no-one else could do
any either. He was particularly fond
of what he called 'barging' – shoulder-
charging smaller boys and sending
them flying.

Jimmy had heard some of the
teachers saying that Paul was
'disruptive' and ought to be sent to a
special school. Jimmy couldn't help
wondering what a school full of Pauls
would be like. But Paul's parents
wouldn't hear of it and somehow Paul
never quite did anything bad enough,
so they seemed to be stuck with him.

Jimmy hurried through the gates

and into the playground to recover his bag. A very small boy called Timmy, usually known as Mouse, the smallest boy in Jimmy's class came running up with it. 'Here you are, Jimmy. I saw where it landed.' Mouse handed over the bag and ran off, too shy to say more.

'Thanks, Mouse!' Jimmy opened the bag and peered inside.

T.R. glared indignantly up at him. His fur looked ruffled and his glasses had been knocked all crooked. He was muttering to himself in his low rumbling voice. 'Of all the gold-durned, hell-fired, tarnation dang-fool tricks!'

'Sorry, T.R.,' whispered Jimmy. He straightened T.R.'s glasses for him. 'Are you all right?'

'I guess so. What the blue blazes –'

Jimmy explained about Paul Ferris.

T.R. snorted. 'You oughta *do* something about that guy. If he keeps on getting away with it, he'll just keep on acting up.'

'That's easy enough to say. You haven't seen the size of him.'

T.R. began muttering things like. 'The bigger they are the harder they fall,' and 'when the going gets tough, the tough get going.'

Jimmy heard the school bell ring. 'Sssh!' he whispered. Popping T.R. back inside the bag, he joined the noisy, chattering, jostling crowd of children heading into the school.

Jimmy went up the one flight of stairs that led to his classroom, hung the satchel and his coat on the peg and gathered round the teacher who was calling the register. Their class leader, Mr Briskin, was a thin, fair rather nervous young man. He was nice enough most of the time, but tended to get into a bit of a flap. Sometimes he exploded alarmingly when things got on top of him.

He was in even more of a fuss than usual this morning because Monday was Dinner Money Day. All those who had school dinners, more or less everyone, had to bring the week's dinner money in an envelope with their name on it.

Jimmy lived near enough to the school to go home for lunch, but he found it better to stay at school. Although everyone grumbled, the food was actually quite good.

Jimmy had tried going home for dinner for a while but it hadn't really worked out. His father was out all day teaching history at a local college. His mother was a potter, with a kiln in a little shed at the bottom of the garden. Trouble was, she got so involved in her work that she forgot the time – including dinner time. Many a day Jimmy had arrived home to find his mother enthusing over some weirdly shaped pot, and no food ready. After a bit he'd decided that the certainty of a school dinner was better than the faint chance of a home-cooked one.

Jimmy put his dinner money in the big round, red cake-tin that served as a safe and went to his usual place.

When the register was called and all the money collected, Mr Briskin put the lid on the tin and put it on the window sill beside his desk.

'Well, as you all know, today's Monday, so welcome back to another exciting week at school.' Everybody groaned.

Mr Briskin went on, 'As you also know, Monday is show and tell day, so who's brought something interesting to show and tell about?'

Jimmy felt suddenly shy and looked round hoping someone else would put his hand up, but nobody did.

Reluctantly, Jimmy raised his
hand.

'Well done,' said Mr Briskin. 'Let's
see it then.'

Jimmy went to his satchel, took out
T.R. Bear, and sat him up on the
table in front of the class.

There was a murmuring from the

class and a few chuckles as T.R. sat there, glaring aggressively at them from behind his glasses.

'How sweet,' said Paul Ferris loudly. 'He's brought his little teddy!'

'Shut up, Paul,' said Mr Briskin wearily. 'Off you go Jimmy!'

Jimmy drew a deep breath. 'Well, as our bright friend at the back spotted at once, this *is* a teddy bear.'

That got quite a good laugh, which made Jimmy feel better, even though

20

Paul glared threateningly at him.

'However, this is a rather unusual teddy bear,' continued Jimmy. 'To begin with, he's an American bear ...'

Jimmy told them about getting T.R. as a present from his Uncle Colin in America. 'Most people think teddy bears are English, because of Winnie-the-Pooh and Rupert and all that sort of thing. But the most likely

explanation seems to be that they were named after Theodore

Roosevelt, who was President of the USA in …' Jimmy trailed off realising he didn't know exactly. From somewhere below him a low voice rumbled, 'Nineteenhunnerdanone.' T.R. was prompting him, though luckily without moving his lips.

'In nineteen hundred and one,' Jimmy went on hurriedly. 'Anyway, people always used to call him Teddy, short for Theodore. The story goes that Teddy Roosevelt was out hunting one day, and the only thing they found was a baby bear that had lost its mother. Teddy Roosevelt refused to shoot it because it was so small. A few days later there was a cartoon about it in the papers. Soon after that a man with a little toyshop in New York made a toy bear and put it in the window. He called it 'Teddy's Bear', and soon he was selling the bears as fast as he could make them. Then the big toymakers joined in ...'

Jimmy went on to tell how teddy bears had become a craze all over the world.

'Very interesting,' said Mr Briskin. 'Thank you, Jimmy. Now, we'd better get on with some work. Take out your English readers please ...'

Jimmy put T.R. Bear up on the window sill beside the money tin thinking it would be more interesting for him there than inside the satchel – then got out his books and started work.

The first lesson went by peacefully enough. It was in the last lesson before break that the trouble started.

'Mental maths,' announced Mr Briskin to another chorus of groans. 'We'll start with a little test on the times table ...'

Jimmy hated these tests. Mr Briskin would shoot some impossible sum at you like seven times eight or eleven times twelve or something and you were expected to rap out the answer just like that.

Jimmy's mind always seemed to go quite blank and sometimes he found himself unable to answer very simple questions – like two times two. He sat there paralysed, hoping Mr Briskin wouldn't point to him first. But he did.

'Jimmy! Nine times seven?'

Jimmy just stared at him, mouth
open.

A loud voice hissed, 'Sixty-three!'

Mr Briskin glared round. 'Who said
that? No helping!'

He pointed to Jimmy again. 'Eight
times eight?'

Jimmy thought furiously. Sixty
something, what was it? Sixty two?
No, that sounded wrong. Sixty-four!
But before he could give the answer
the same mysterious voice muttered,
'Sixty-four!'

Mr Briskin jumped to his feet. 'Stop that at once. No helping, I said no helping and I mean it!'

He glared round the class trying to see which boy the voice was coming from.

He just couldn't work it out – and Jimmy knew why. The voice wasn't coming from a boy at all. It was coming from T.R. Bear on the window sill just behind Mr Briskin's head.

Mr Briskin was on the brink of one of his famous rages. 'I warn you, if this happens one more time, I shall keep the whole class in at break!'

Jimmy knew he had to do something. He raised his voice, speaking very loudly and clearly. 'Please don't do that, Mr Briskin. I expect whoever's trying to help me means well, but I don't want them to do it, and I wish they'd stop!'

As he spoke these last words, Jimmy looked hard at T.R. up on the window sill.

He could have sworn he saw the bear give a tiny shrug.

'Right,' said Mr Briskin, trembling a little. 'We'll try again. Seven threes?'

Luckily this was an easy one, and Jimmy said thankfully, 'Twenty-one!'

Mr Briskin went on round the class, but as T.R. didn't seem bothered about helping anyone else, the rest of the test finished without any more fuss.

The bell for morning break rang, and Jimmy gave a sigh of relief.

What he still didn't realise was, that the day's problems were just beginning.

Chapter Three

The Robbery

Jimmy went to the window and pretended to straighten up T.R., though he really just wanted to have a quick word with him.

'What do you think you're playing at, T.R.? You promised not to talk when anyone could hear.'

'Sorry kid. I just got carried away!'

'You nearly got us all kept in. I'm going to leave you right here on the shelf till after break. Try not to get into any more trouble! And whatever you do, *don't* move or talk!'

He turned and followed the others down the stairs into the playground.

Some of his friends were playing football and Jimmy joined in, dashing about with the rest all over the playground. He had just booted the ball between the two chalk-marks on the wall that served as goal-posts when a heavy hand fell on his shoulder.

'Hey, you!'

Jimmy turned and saw Paul Ferris looming over him. He looked sort of nervous and excited all at the same time. And for some reason he was determined to make a fuss.

He gripped Jimmy's shoulder. 'You were making fun of me in class!"As our bright friend at the back spotted,

29

it's a teddy bear!" What do you mean, making a fool out of me?'

Jimmy seemed to hear T.R.'s voice in his ear. 'Walk softly – and carry a big stick,' T.R. had said. 'Don't look for trouble, but be ready to handle it if it comes.' He pulled away from Paul's grip. 'Make a fool of *you*, Paul? No need for me to do that, nature's done it already!'

There was a yell of laughter from Jimmy's friends.

Since Paul was fairly dim, it took a moment for the insult to sink in. Then, with a yell of rage he charged straight at Jimmy, clearly intending to 'barge' him into the wall.

But this time Jimmy was ready. He wasn't big, but he was nippy, and although he didn't have a big stick he did have a foot. Leaping aside he stuck his foot out. Paul tripped, missed Jimmy completely, and barged straight into the wall instead.

'Ouch!' he yelled. My hand, my hand. Look, it's bleeding. Get a doctor!'

For a moment Jimmy wondered if Paul was really hurt. Then he saw he'd just grazed his knuckles on the wall. Painful enough to be sure, but hardly fatal.

Paul went on yelling and Mr Briskin came running up. He was on break duty that day, which meant he was in a bad temper to start with – Mr Briskin *hated* break duty. 'All right, all right, what's all the fuss about?'

Jimmy said, 'We were just mucking about, Sir. Paul tripped and fell into the wall. He's hurt his hand.'

Mr Briskin examined the graze. 'Good heavens boy, that won't kill you. Go and wash it then go and see the school secretary, she'll put a plaster on it for you.'

Still snivelling, Paul went off.

Nick, one of Jimmy's friends, slapped him on the back. 'Well done, Jimmy, you showed him. About time someone stood up to him.'

'He'll murder you when he feels better, though,' warned someone else.

'Let him try,' said Jimmy trying not to sound scared. Then suddenly he realised that he really *wasn't* scared. Paul didn't seem so frightening now that a grazed hand had reduced him to a jelly.

Anyway, he'd started it. Jimmy frowned. Come to think of it, it was unlike Paul to make a big public fuss like that. Barge and run was more his usual line. He looked thoughtfully after Paul, who had reached the school door by now. He was standing talking to someone. It was Mouse. Funny that, thought Jimmy. Paul was

meaner to Mouse than anyone else so they were hardly friends. Yet somehow Jimmy got the impression Mouse was waiting for Paul …

'Come on,' said Nick. 'We've still got a couple of minutes. Let's get on with the game.'

After break they all filed back into the classroom.

Paul came in last displaying a big sticking plaster on his hand.

Jimmy sat down. It was drawing, then story time. Not too bad at all.

He heard a voice mutter. 'Kid! Hey kid! I gotta talk to you.' It was T.R.

Jimmy looked up at the window. T.R. was sitting quite still staring straight ahead, and his lips weren't moving. All the same the whisper came again. 'Kid! You *gotta* listen!'

'Sssh!' hissed Jimmy desperately. 'Shut up, T.R.!'

Mr Briskin looked round suspiciously. 'Stop all that talking whoever it is. Now, get out your art things.'

All at once there came a tremendous crash.

Mr Briskin jumped about a foot in the air, and whirled round.

The big red money tin had fallen

from the window sill and crashed to the ground. It rolled across the room.

T.R. had fallen from the window sill too, and Jimmy ran to pick him up. As he sat him back on the sill he

whispered furiously, 'What are you up to T.R.? *You* pushed that tin off, over-balanced and fell off after it.'

'I hadda get your attention. Somebody's cracked your crib and snatched the loot. The dinner dough's gone.'

'Are you sure?'

'Happened right in front of me.'

'Why didn't you stop them?'

'How? Anyway, you said I wasn't to move or talk, remember?'

'Did you see who it was?'

'Little kid, glasses and big ears …'

'Mouse!' Jimmy couldn't believe it. Mouse was the last person to steal anything. Now if it had been Paul Ferris, that would be different.

Jimmy thought hard. What was he going to do? He didn't want to get Mouse into trouble, but all the same …

Suddenly he heard a shout from Mr Briskin who had picked up the tin, realised it was strangely light and looked inside. 'The dinner money's gone!'

There was a babble of astonishment

and shock, and everyone gathered round to look at Mr Briskin holding the empty tin.

Everyone except Jimmy. He stayed where he was. He looked at Mouse, who seemed quite terrified, and at Paul who was looking smug, and all at once everything fell into place.

Paul's picking on him in the playground, his whispered conversation with Mouse – suddenly it all made sense.

Thanks to T.R.'s help and his own bright idea, Jimmy felt certain he knew who was really guilty. But how was he going to prove it?

Chapter Four

The Magic Bear

'Everybody be quiet and go back to your places,' shouted Mr Briskin. 'I'm trying to think what to do next.' He looked even more nervous than usual. Jimmy could easily guess why, and Mr Briskin's next words proved him right. 'I'm afraid this is partly my fault. Dinner money is supposed to be handed into the school office at break, but I was on break duty today and I'm afraid I forgot. I don't know what

Miss Keen is going to say.'

Miss Keen was the Headmistress, a large fierce lady who terrified the staff even more than she did the pupils.

'Now,' Mr Briskin went on, 'there's nothing to *prove* someone in this class took the money. Anybody could have walked in. But we have to admit that there's at least a chance it was one of us. We knew the money was in the tin, and one of us could have gone in and out without anyone taking any notice. A stranger, or even someone from another class might be spotted. So, first of all, does anyone want to own up?'

There was a moment of silence then everyone started talking at once.

'It wasn't me, sir!'

'Wasn't me!'

'It *couldn't* have been me,' shouted

Paul Ferris. 'I was outside all break. You remember I had that fuss with Jimmy, when he shoved me into the wall and I hurt my hand. You saw me, Sir.'

Paul was establishing his alibi.

'Well,' said Mr Briskin, 'I shall have to ask everyone to let me look in their pockets and their bags. You must search me and my desk as well. And if that doesn't produce results I'll have to tell Miss Keen, and I suppose she'll have to tell the police!'

'You can search *me* any time,' shouted Paul Ferris. He started turning out his pockets.

Jimmy knew that somehow he had to prove the truth. But how? You couldn't ask a teddy bear to give evidence in court …

Then Jimmy had an idea. 'Listen

to me,' he shouted. 'I think I know how to find out who took the money.'

Mr Briskin gave him a helpless look.

'What do you mean? Find out how?'

'With T.R.'

'With a *teddy bear*?'

Jimmy was thinking fast. 'Well, you see there's a family legend about T.R. He's a magic bear. You can use him to find out the truth.'

'For heaven's sake, Jimmy ...'

'At least let me try. It'll only take a minute, and think of all the horrible fuss it might save us.'

Before Mr Briskin could object, Jimmy ran and took T.R. from the window sill.

As he was lifting him down T.R. whispered, 'What's the plan, kiddo?

What do I do?'

'Just take your cue from me – and when I squeeze you – speak!'

Jimmy held up T.R. in front of the class. 'The legend says that T.R. can sniff out evil-doers. When he finds the guilty person – the bear will speak!'

Holding T.R. in front of him Jimmy began walking around the class. Everyone sat quite still, not really believing anything would happen, but somehow impressed by Jimmy's solemn manner and T.R.'s scowling face.

Jimmy passed child after child, then came to a stop in front of Mouse, who was quivering with fear.

Jimmy hesitated. He wasn't looking forward to this bit, but it had to be done.

He held T.R. out in front of him,

pushing him towards Mouse, who sat there as if hypnotised. When T.R. was so close to Mouse that no-one else could see or hear, he gave T.R. a squeeze.

The astonished Mouse saw T.R. come to life.

The bear stared straight into his eyes and growled softly, 'Okay kid, come clean and we'll go easy on you. I was there, remember? *I saw you take the money.*'

Mouse burst into tears. 'All right, all right,' he sobbed. 'It was me. But it wasn't my idea. He made me do it.'

Mr Briskin hurried forward. 'Made you? Who made you?'

'Stop!' shouted Jimmy. 'The magic bear says there is another guilty one here. The real criminal. We must sniff him out!'

Holding T.R. out in front of him, Jimmy headed straight for Paul Ferris, who jumped up and backed away into a corner.

Jimmy ran after him, penning him in. He held up T.R., thrusting him forward till Paul and T.R. were practically nose to nose.

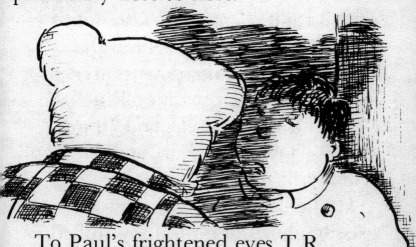

To Paul's frightened eyes T.R. seemed to grow in size till he looked more like a real grizzly than a teddy bear.

Jimmy gave T.R. a squeeze.

T.R. scowled fiercely into Paul's frightened face. *'Okay, fatso!'* he growled in a fierce James Cagney voice. *'We got the goods on you, you dirty rat! Squeal, before I give you the woiks!'*

Paul Ferris gave a yell of fear. 'Help, help, get him off me! It was me all right, I made Mouse do it. The money's hidden behind the heating pipes in the downstairs cloakroom. Just get him off me!'

'It's all right, Paul,' said Jimmy gently. 'T.R. can't hurt you. He's only a teddy bear.'

He held up T.R. who stared glassily ahead of him, a toy stuffed bear once again. That was more or less the end of that, though there was still quite a bit more fuss to come.

Mr Briskin took Paul Ferris and

Mouse to see Miss Keen, who soon
got full confessions out of both of
them.

Paul had been stealing money and sweets from Mouse for some time. When there was no more to steal he had terrified Mouse into stealing the dinner money and hiding it, so that Paul could pick it up later.

Since the money was all recovered Miss Keen decided against calling the police. Mouse was let off with a fairly gentle telling off – Miss Keen was quite kind-hearted really – and sent home for the day because *he* was so upset. Paul Ferris was sent home too – permanently. Miss Keen said she would make arrangements for him to go to a special school, and if he or his parents made any fuss she might change her mind about telling the police.

At the end of the day everyone crowded round Jimmy, wanting to know how he'd done it. Mr Briskin said worriedly, 'That bear can't *really* talk – can it?'

Luckily, Jimmy had his answers ready. 'No, of course not. I guessed it must be Mouse because he looked so scared, and I saw Paul talking to him later and guessed he was behind it – Mouse is too nice and too timid to steal. But that's all it was – guesswork. No proof. I used the bear to scare the truth out of them, I just held up the bear and spoke from behind it in a deep voice!'

Mr Briskin accepted the story with relief. After all, it was so much more believable than the truth!

On the way home they stopped for a rest on the park bench. Jimmy took T.R. out of the satchel and sat him on the bench beside him.

'Well, kid, that was quite a day,' growled T.R. 'I thought you told me school life was dull?'

Jimmy gave the bear a hug. 'I should have known better, shouldn't I, T.R.? Nothing's ever dull when you're around!'

T.R. BEAR: ENTER T.R.

BY TERRANCE DICKS

It all started when Jimmy got a parcel from his Uncle Colin in America. The teddy bear inside was unlike any bear Jimmy had ever seen. He looked tough, and he was wearing glasses! According to the label, his name was Theodore Roosevelt—T.R. for short.

And life with T.R. is quite eventful as Jimmy and the other toys soon find out.

This is the first in a series of books about T.R.

0 552 523011

YOUNG CORGI

T.R. BEAR: T.R.'S DAY OUT

BY TERRANCE DICKS

When Jimmy's school arranges a day trip to a museum, T.R. and the other toys insist Jimmy takes them along with him. There are lots of things they want to see too!

With T.R. along, Jimmy's trip becomes the most exciting day out ever!

This is the third in a series of books about T.R.

0 552 523569

YOUNG CORGI

T.R. BEAR: T.R. AFLOAT

BY TERRANCE DICKS

*'Sixteen men on a dead man's chest,' sang T.R. Bear.
'Yo ho ho and a bottle of rum!'*

Jimmy and T.R. are on holiday at last. On a
boat! The drive down and the first night on
board are quite an adventure in themselves.
But there's more excitement in store when T.R.
overhears two men plotting to steal some rare
birds' eggs from the island nature reserve.

He's determined to catch them red-handed. All
he needs is a plan . . .

0 552 524654

YOUNG CORGI

URSULA SAILING

BY SHEILA LAVELLE
ILLUSTRATED BY THELMA LAMBERT

Ursula is an ordinary girl – with one very special secret. She can turn herself into a real, live, little bear! Sometimes this can be very useful, especially when there is a tall and difficult tree to climb. But in this new adventure for Ursula, she soon discovers that rivers and boats mean trouble for bears . . .

0 552 524484

YOUNG
CORGI

URSULA CAMPING

BY SHEILA LAVELLE
ILLUSTRATED BY THELMA LAMBERT

Ursula is an ordinary girl – with one special difference. If she eats a currant bun, stuffed with a mixture of porridge oats and honey, and recites a magic spell, she can turn herself into a real, live, little bear!

When she runs up against trouble from her two cousins, Ian and Jamie, while on a camping holiday in the New Forest, Ursula finds that being able to change herself into a bear can be very useful indeed . . .

0 552 524476

YOUNG CORGI

If you would like to receive a Newsletter about our new Children's books, just fill in the coupon below with your name and address (or copy it onto a separate piece of paper if you don't want to spoil your book) and send it to:

**The Children's Books Editor
Young Corgi Books
61-63 Uxbridge Road,
Ealing
London W5 5SA**

Please send me a Children's Newsletter:

Name..

Address..

....

....

All Children's Books are available at your bookshop or newsagent, or can be ordered from the following address:
Corgi/Bantam Books,
Cash Sales Department,
P.O. Box 11, Falmouth, Cornwall TR10 9 EN

Please send a cheque or postal order (no currency) and allow 60p for postage and packing for the first book plus 25p for the second book and 15p for each additional book ordered up to a maximum charge of £1.90 in UK.

B.F.P.O. customers please allow 60p for the first book, 25p for the second book plus 15p per copy for the next 7 books, thereafter 9p per book.

Overseas customers, including Eire, please allow £1.25 for postage and packing for the first book, 75p for the second book, and 28p for each subsequent title ordered.